Show Time!

Written by Suzy Senior

Illustrated by Monika Róża Wiśniewska

Collins

T0321566

There will be a show to find new talent at school.

The children make a few posters to put up.

Super Talent Show!
Friday

Each child thinks of what they would like to do:

play the flute

demonstrate judo

a juggling display

make music in a group

5

Some pupils make their own costumes.
The teachers help out.

smart suit

brushes

blue and yellow card

glitter glue

tape

paint

pipe cleaners

glue stick

7

The children go over their acts. They should be super by Friday!

8

The staff decorate the venue.

spotlights

streamers

posters

rows of seats

9

Hooray! It is time! The show is due to start.

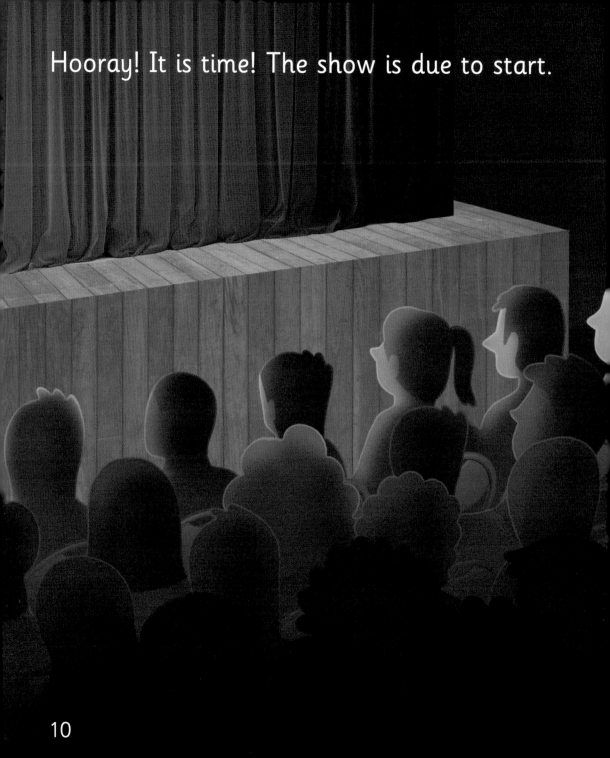

The seats are full. All the pupils and grown-ups are here.

At the start, this duo performs a tango.

Next, a group of friends boogie to disco music, with bright lights.

This child plays the tuba!
His friend plays a tune on the flute.

Next, we have a judo display.

judo suit

blue belt

crash mats

And what's the final act? Look at the clues:

Blue wig?

Red nose?

Yes! The teachers have hired clown suits.
They are quite brave!

A clown just threw a bucket of streamers over the crowd!

The music teacher plays one final tune.
It's time to take a bow.

The grown-ups clap and go wild.
What a superb talent show!

What would you like to do?

After reading

Letters and Sounds: Phase 5

Word count: 234

Focus phonemes: /ai/ ay, a-e, ey /ee/ ea, ie /igh/ i, i-e /oa/ o, ow, o-e /oo/ u, ue, ew, ui, ou, u-e /oo/ oul

Common exception words: out, all, there, here, some, of, to, the, put, full, are, be, by, one, have, do, what, school, their, friends, we

Curriculum links: Music: listen with concentration and understanding to a range of high-quality live and recorded music; Physical education: perform dances using simple movement patterns

National Curriculum learning objectives: Reading/word reading: read other words of more than one syllable that contain taught GPCs; read common exception words, noting unusual correspondences between spelling and sound and where these occur in the word; Reading/comprehension: drawing on what they already know or on background information and vocabulary provided by the teacher; understand both the books they can already read accurately and fluently and those they listen to by checking that the text makes sense to them as they read, and correcting inaccurate reading

Developing fluency

- Your child may enjoy hearing you read the book.
- Take turns reading a page. Check that your child notices and pauses at commas and uses a more excited tone for sentences ending in exclamation marks.

Phonic practice

- Focus on spellings of /oo/ and /ee/ sounds. Ask your child to sound out and blend the following words. Can they identify which word has both sounds? (*boogie*)

  cleaners   few   group   each   clues   you   boogie

- Can your child identify the unusual spellings of sounds in these common exception words?

  /oo/ in **to**   /igh/ in **by**   /e/ in **friends**

Extending vocabulary

- Look at page 3 and point to the words **a few**. Ask: Can you think of a word with an opposite meaning? (e.g. *lots, masses, loads*)
- Repeat for the following:

  page 8 **super** (e.g. *awful, dreadful, terrible*)   page 18 **brave** (e.g. *terrified, scared, timid*)